Table of Contents

Table of Contents 1

Thanks 2

Introduction 3

Chapter 1 4

Chapter 2 12

Chapter 3 24

Chapter 4: Plasmic 36

Chapter 5: Micheal 37

Chapter 6 42

Chapter 7 45

Chapter 8 54

Chapter 9: Logan 57

Chapter 10: Micheal 59

Sneak Peak of The Soldier Lost 63

Message from the Author 64

Thanks

Thanks to my Mom for giving me the idea for writing about my brother's and my adventures in our woods. From that idea, grew a love of writing. Thanks to my Dad for helping me plan out what I needed to do for my stories, and for helping me copyright *Two Soldiers*. Thanks to God for giving me the inspiration and helping me become more creative. Thanks to Andy for helping me critique and edit out grammatical errors, and for supporting the T.S series from the beginning. Thanks to Kelly, Justin, and Anna for reading and supporting *Two Soldiers.* And thank you reader for helping me live my dream. Keep Calm and Dream On!!!

Introduction

My name is Micheal Joule. I have ADHD and Aspergers. I have a younger brother named Logan, and it's because of Logan that I'm telling you this. You see, I might look like everyone else, but unlike everyone else, I have a gift. Not a gift as in talent, but as in a power. I can control and absorb positive electricity and plasma. This gift wasn't something that I was born with, no it literally was a gift. Now you're probably wondering how I got this gift, so I'll tell you.

To start, I'll give you an explanation of what I am. I'm what is known as a half-brother. A half-brother is a human who has their DNA fused with a being able to control an element of nature. There have been a few half-brothers throughout history, some you may have heard of, like Thor. But most half-brothers tend to keep their powers secret, to avoid the stress and focus of the spotlight.

Most half-brothers, including myself, are twelve when they receive their 'gift'. Some may get it at fifteen, others at eight. But for the most part, twelve is the preferred age. Why this is, is unknown. Some think it's because the body is more acceptable to change, others think it's because of a tradition, and then there are those who say "Who cares? We have super powers."

There is much more to say about half-brothers, but everything I've mentioned is pretty much the basics. Now, I'll tell you about how I got my 'gift'.

Chapter 1

It started January 30, 2009, my twelfth birthday. That was the day Logan started talking about little black creatures in our woods. He called them Black-ts, and was paranoid about them taking over the world, or something like that. He kept trying to get me to go down into the woods with him, and after school on Thursday February 12, finally succeeded.

"It's about time you believe me," Logan said as he led me to our woods.

"I'm not doing this because I believe you, I'm doing this so you'll shut up," I said. We entered the woods, and Logan signaled me to be quiet and aware of my surroundings. I stopped walking, and closed my eyes, listening to my surroundings. *Look behind you.* My eyes shot open, and I spun around. *Up here.* I looked up and saw a creature that resembled a red-eyed tree frog. *How old are you?*

"Twelve," I said.

"Twelve what?" asked Logan.

"Didn't you hear, the frog-thing asked my age," I said as I turned to Logan.

"Frog-thing? Where'd you see a frog-thing?" asked Logan.

"Up there," I said as I pointed to where it was.

"I don't see anything," said Logan.

"But it's clear as..." I looked where the creature was, but saw nothing "...where'd it go?"

"Maybe you're just seeing things," laughed Logan.

"You're one to talk," I said. Logan turned around and signaled me to follow. About an hour had past, when he suddenly put his back to a tree.

"Hide!" he whispered urgently. I ran to a tree to the side of him.

"What are we hiding from?" I asked silently.

"Them," said Logan as he pointed behind him. I looked in the direction he was pointing, and saw two figures. I suddenly became overwhelmed with curiosity. I crept closer and closer to the figures, until I was able to get a better look at them. The figure closest to me was human, but the other one was probably about three feet tall and pitch black. The smaller figure had a weird, red pattern on its chest in the shape of a "T", and had red eyes.

"What are you doing? Don't let them see you, or else they might hurt us... or kill us," said Logan silently.

"Did you hear something?" the human asked.

"N-no," said the short figure.

"As I was saying, the Wilsons have denied Siphe for the last time, now Siphe will take the girl by force," the human said.

"H-how d-do you p-plan on d-doing t-that?" asked the short figure.

"It's simple: their car will be passing these woods in a few days; I need you and your buddies to make that car crash without killing the girl; I'll stall the godparents while my comrade picks her up from the hospital. If everything goes according to my plan, I'll give your leader the siphoning slime," said the human.

"Siphoning slime?" I said, a little too loud. The human spun around, while the short figure froze. Logan pulled a foldable baton out his pocket (I'm not sure why he had it in the first place).

"Are you still good with a sword?" Logan asked me.

"With five years of training? Of course I am!" I asked. Logan pulled a sword from behind his back.

"Here, I'll hold off the man while you go after the black-t," Logan said as he handed me the sword. Then Logan got the man's attention while I ran towards the black-t. The black-t turned around and ran. I followed it to a bridge over a small pond. When I got to the bridge, I saw that it had fallen apart from old age. Only half of the bridge was still intact, and at the edge of the bridge was the black-t.

I got on the bridge, and pointed my sword at the black-t. It frantically looked from side to side. It started shaking and slowly backed up. It seemed to have fear, something Logan said black-ts didn't have. The black-t pulled out a knife and swung it around, but lost its grip and the knife flew into the pond. It looked at me and my sword, and closed its eyes and turned its head away. It knew I followed it to kill it.

I looked at my sword and then to the black-t, who was shaking with fear. *Am I really going to kill something that's defenseless? It's probably more scared of me than I am of it.* I dropped my sword and the black-t looked at me with a nervous curiosity.

"A-are you l-letting me go?" the black-t asked.

"I don't know, maybe," I said.

"T-then w-why d-did you d-drop your sword?" the black-t asked.

"Because I can't kill you, I'd have nightmares," I said. The sound of a wolf's howl made both of us jump. The black-t took a step backwards. There was a loud snap, and the black-t fell into the pond. I ran to the edge of the bridge and saw that it had somehow managed to land on its feet. It started to scream as the water around its feet began to fizz.

Hopefully this isn't a pond full of acid. I jumped into the water, grabbed the black-t, and pulled the both of us back up unto the bridge. I looked at the black-t to see that half its legs had dissolved in the water. It was losing blood, so I tore the sleeves off my shirt. I wrapped the sleeves tightly around both of its legs. *Move to the side of the bridge.* As soon I moved to the side, a red beam hit the black-t. Suddenly, the sleeves disappeared, and the veins connected to the arteries. The bleeding had stopped and the black-t's legs began to glow, as they slowly started to grow back.

Then I heard a snarl, and I turned around to see a wolf covered in leaves, with its teeth bearing. I signaled the black-t to stay, as I slowly walked to my sword. After grabbing my sword, I slowly backed up to the black-t.

"W-what are you d-doing?" the black-t asked nervously.

"Protecting you, that's what," I said.

"W-why? I h-haven't d-done an-anything to h-help you," the black-t said confused.

"You don't have to, and why would I save you just to let you die a few seconds later?" I asked, as I looked at the black-t. The black-t stared at me and its eyes changed from red to blue. I looked back at the wolf, who started to slowly approach me. I tightened my grip on the sword and aimed it at the wolf.

"Move away boy, this doesn't concern you," said the wolf. I was caught a little off guard by hearing it speak, but still stood my ground.

"I think it does," I said, "So go away and you'll live."

"You've got guts kid," said the wolf, "I'm going to enjoy spilling them." The wolf charged at me, and I readied myself. The wolf leaped and I thrust my sword forward as it tackled me. The wolf became limp, so I pushed it off of me to get up.

"See, if you would've just walked away, you'd still be alive," I said to the wolf's limp body.

"Oh, I'm alive, something you soon won't be able to say about yourself," said the wolf. I looked at the wolf's body and a chill went down my spine, as it is slowly got back up.

"What are you?" I asked nervously.

"I'm a leaf wolf, and your weapons of man don't affect me," it said. *Weapons of man?* I looked at my sword and realized what the leaf wolf meant. I dropped my sword and put up my fists.

"What about the hands of man?" I asked. The leaf wolf snarled at me.

"You won't be fast enough to use your fists," the leaf wolf growled, "Prepare yourself, the odds of surviving this are very low." I immediately regretted jumping into the cold water, as my limbs felt stiff from the plunge. The leaf wolf leaped at me again, and tackled me before I could react. It bit at me and tried to get my neck. I put my arms over my neck and face, but it took advantage of my act of self-defense and bit both of my arms. Its bite grew tighter and tighter. I felt a warm liquid drip on my face and neck, and realized it was my blood.

I struggled to break the leaf wolf's grip, but failed. I began to lose strength and energy. As a last resort to break the grip, I kicked the leaf wolf in the stomach. The leaf wolf released my arms, and I grabbed it. With the last of my strength, I pushed the leaf wolf off of me.

"Ha-ha ha, I told you that you probably wouldn't survive this," the leaf wolf laughed, "But before I kill you, I'm going to kill your friend and you're going to watch him die." The leaf wolf tightly bit my right shoulder and threw me against the side of the bridge. I looked at the black-t and saw the fear in his eyes. My ADHD kicked in, and energy filled my body. I managed to get up onto my feet and got between the black-t and the leaf wolf.

"Y-you're not going to harm this black-t while I'm still alive," I said.

"Alright, you can die first," said the leaf wolf, as it ran at me again. That's when my Aspergers kicked in. Everything (seemed to have) slowed down, as I started to think ahead. I saw almost every move I could make and the outcome that would follow. I glanced over to where the leaf wolf had thrown me, and saw a crack in the wood. *Perfect.* Everything sped back up, and the leaf wolf leaped, but I caught it. I used its own momentum to throw it into the cracked part of the bridge. There was a loud snap and the leaf wolf went into the water.

"Time to run," I said to the black-t. We ran to solid ground and were running for about five minutes, when all of the sudden, we started to hear howl after howl. The black-t stopped running.

"St-stop, t-they'll kill you, I'm who t-they want," said the black-t, "I a-appre-appreciate what you've d-done to protect me, b-but I won't pay you b-back by letting you die."

"I won't die, I promise," I said, "Now, do you know how to climb a tree?"

"Yes, b-but I d-don't see how that could save us," said the black-t.

"Not us, just you," I said, "Now go climb a tree."

"B-but what about you?" the black-t asked as he climbed up a tree.

"What's your name?" I asked.

"Alex," he answered.

"Well, Alex, this won't be the last time you'll see me," I said. Once Alex was pretty high up, I turned around and ran, making as much noise as I could. *Not much energy plus minor hypothermia plus a pack of homicidal wolves equals very poor odds for me. I must be crazy.* I was soon surrounded by leaf wolves.

"Where's the black-t, boy?" asked a leaf wolf.

"I'll die before I tell you," I said.

"Have it your way," said another leaf wolf, "Kill him!" The leaf wolves started to circle around me, and the sweet smell of chloroform filled the air. I started to feel light headed, and energy began to leave my body. I began to stagger around and struggled to keep balance. Suddenly, there was a sharp pain in my left leg. I fell to the ground. A leaf wolf approached me.

"You had your whole life ahead of you, but you decided to throw it away for someone so worthless," said the leaf wolf.

"Nobody's worthless," I said weakly.

"I'm going to enjoy watching you die," said the leaf wolf. A leaf wolf bit my left shoulder and threw me across the ground.

"You see, black-ts weren't always evil. Their creator, Boss-T, originally intended them to help mankind, but we leaf wolves didn't like that. We hate mankind, so we corrupted the heart of Boss-T with the lust of power. He started to create the black-ts to rule over fellow man, but sometimes a black-t will be created with emotions. Those rare black-ts have the capability to ruin everything we've done, so they must die," said the leaf wolf who threw me. Another leaf wolf bit my right leg, spun around, and threw me farther. I slammed into a tree and heard the crack of some of my ribs. It became painful to breathe.

I struggled to keep my eyes open. I tried to get up, but didn't have the strength. *Hold on, help is on the way, look up.* I looked up, and saw the frog-thing, who had wings and was flying. I heard a screech, as the frog-thing landed between me and the leaf wolves. *Don't be afraid, you'll receive no harm from me.* The frog-thing made a weird sound, and more frog-things appeared. Soon, the frog-things outnumbered the leaf wolves. The frog-things fought off the leaf wolves, while the first one got closer to me. Then, everything went black.

Chapter 2

When I awoke, I was in a bed. *What a crazy dream.* I got up and looked around. I felt an itch on my right shoulder, but when I went to scratch it, I felt an odd cloth. I pulled my shirt away from my shoulder and saw my shoulder wrapped in what seemed to be medical wrap. *Oh my gosh, it did happen.* I took another look around and saw a door. I ran to the door, opened it, and saw frog-things.

"*Good to see you're okay,*" said a deep voice.

"Who said that?" I asked nervously. A frog-thing stepped forward.

"*I did,*" said the voice.

"Where are you?" I asked.

"*In front of you, I'm the 'frog-thing',*" said the frog-thing, "*I'm telepathic, and the leader of my race, known as the frids. My name is Keveal-Chard.*"

"Why am I here?" I asked.

"*You are here because we chose you,*" said Keveal-Chard, "*You will be given a power that few have had.*"

"You chose me? Why? And what do you mean by 'power that few have had'?" I asked.

"*We chose you because of your heart, and selflessness. The power is the ability to control and absorb electricity and plasma,*" Keveal-Chard explained. I was dumbfounded. I couldn't believe that I was about to become a superhero.

"When do I get this power?" I asked.

"*As soon as you tell us which charge you want: positive or negative?*" Keveal-Chard asked.

"Umm, I choose positive," I said.

"*Good choice, follow me,*" said Keveal-Chard. I followed Keveal-Chard to a room without a roof. I looked up at the sky to see it full of thunderclouds. Yellow and blue lightning danced from cloud to cloud. Keveal-Chard made a crackling noise and lightning struck the floor next to him. When the lightning went away, a four-legged creature stood next to Keveal-Chard. The creature was blue, with a yellow lightning pattern. Three of the creature's legs were normal. The fourth leg was thicker than the others, and was brightly glowing golden-yellow.

Then the strangest thing happened, the creature got up on its hind-legs and became humanoid. The creature held out its right hand. *Shake his hand.* I grabbed his hand with my right hand, but lost all control of it before I could shake it. Lightning struck the humanoid creature and I felt the worst pain I've ever felt. My vision became odd, switching back and forth from normal to the electricity in front of me.

I looked at my right arm and saw the shape of plasma appear on top of it, in the form of what seemed to be scar tissue. When the 'scar' reached my elbow, I immediately felt weak. The creature put his left hand on my right arm and I felt strength slowly come back to my body. When the creature removed his left hand, the scar was dimly glowing blue. The pain slowly started to lessen. When the pain was gone, I regained control of my right arm.

The creature let go of my arm and aimed his arm at me. Lightning shot out of his hand and struck me. The weird part was that it didn't hurt, in fact it actually felt great.

"What is your name, brother?" asked a monotone voice.

"Micheal, but I also go by Mike," I said.

"Well, Mike, you're now my half-brother, and in need of an electro name," said the voice, "Hence forth, you shall be known as Plasmike."

"So now I have two brothers? Sweet! Wait, you never told me your name," I said.

"I am Plasmic, and I'll teach you how to use your powers," said Plasmic, "Follow me." I followed Plasmic outside, to find the grass and the leaves of the trees glowing, and switching from yellow to red to blue to purple to black to white to orange.

"Where are we?" I asked.

"Didn't Keveal tell you, you're on Planet Electro," said Plasmic.

"Planet Electro?" I asked.

"Yes, and don't worry, when it's time for you to go back to Earth, only a minute will have passed," said Plasmic, "Now, before we start your training, keep in mind that lightning now courses through your veins. Electricity is now your lifeline and as long as you have it in your electrical supply, blood and oxygen are secondary. To begin your first lesson, electricity comes in many forms, all of which can be found here on Planet Electro: close your eyes, and focus on the electricity around you." I did what he said, and within a matter of seconds, I saw and felt the electricity in the grass and in the leaves of the trees.

"Wow, this is amazing," I said, "wait, why'd everything disappear?"

"Only negative electricity is showing," said Plasmic, "Lesson two: in times of extreme negativity, staying positive can help you see. Keep your eyes closed, and focus on making a pulse of positive static electricity around you." I focused on making a pulse. I quickly felt something leave my right arm, and a second later, my surroundings became lined with yellow electricity.

"Good," said Plasmic, "Now open your eyes." I opened my eyes, but still only saw the electricity around me.

"Nothing happened," I said.

"Focus on your other vision," said Plasmic. I focused on my human sight and it slowly started to come back.

"Whoa," I said, "Wait, will I always have to focus to switch from one sight to the other?"

"Well, your brain is different from the others, so you'll probably have to focus for the next three times," said Plasmic.

"There are others like me?" I asked, "And what does my brain being different have to do with anything?"

"No, there were others like you," said Plasmic, "One good example might be Hercules. As for your brain, it adapts to everything and any situation faster than normal."

"Well, that's probably because my brain is super-charged with electricity," I said.

"Your brain did that before you got your powers, now that your brain is super-charged, it'll adapt seven times faster," said Plasmic, "That's why what I'm about to do to you has to be before your brain fully adapts to the electricity, so come quickly." I followed Plasmic into what looked like a small hut. The inside of the hut was full of what seemed to be different metal orbs. Plasmic looked around and zapped a few of the orbs. When he was done, the orbs started to levitate and floated towards each other.

As soon as the orbs made contact with each other, they began to spin at a high speed. The orbs started to glow red, and got closer and closer until they became one.

"What's that?" I asked, pointing to the orb.

"That is the Orb of Conduct," said Plasmic, "But there is one metal that I must add to it." Plasmic went to the wall in front of me, and looked up. Above him was a shelf with a chest.

"Switch to your Electro Sight, I want you to see this," said Plasmic. I focused for a few seconds and my normal vision faded away.

"Okay," I said. I looked at Plasmic, and saw him morph into an electrical form. His form became fuzzy and shot to the shelf. When Plasmic grabbed the chest, he shot back to the ground. He was in his humanoid form when he landed.

"You can switch back to your normal vision now," said Plasmic. I focused again, and my Electro Sight faded away. Plasmic opened the chest and pulled out a glowing, golden-yellow orb. The Orb of Conduct floated to Plasmic, who grabbed it with his free hand. He brought the two orbs closer to each other. The golden-yellow orb began to dissolve into small yellow particles. The particles flew towards the Orb of Conduct, and fused with it, causing it to glow.

After the two orbs fused together, Plasmic gestured me to follow him. We exited the small hut, and went to an area full of sand. Lightning struck the ground in front of us, and two red humanoid creatures approached us. Plasmic got in front of me.

"You're trespassing on Proto Territory," said the creatures in unison.

"I don't want any trouble, I just wish to borrow your sand for about ten minutes," said Plasmic.

"You have ten minutes to use our sand, after that, you must leave," said the creatures in unison, as they flew back into the clouds.

"Okay, we don't have much time. Lay down on your back, and rotate your right arm so that the palm of your hand faces up," said Plasmic. I did what he said and I felt something beneath me push me up. I rose four feet off the ground. Plasmic put sand on my right elbow and hand. Then he raised the orb toward the sky. Suddenly, white lightning struck the orb and Plasmic put the orb above my right arm.

The sand on my hand and elbow turned to glass restraints. Plasmic touched the orb to my skin. I felt pain similar to what I felt when I shook Plasmic's hand, only this time, it was all over my body. I glimpsed at my right arm and saw scar tissue form in the shape of lightning. Only, this time, when the scar tissue reached my elbow, the pain moved to my bones. The orb started to shrink, and Plasmic, with his free hand, covered my mouth.

Every bone, except for my teeth, began to feel like something was forcing its way into every layer. Then, the pain disappeared. I looked at my right arm to see the scar tissue glowing yellow, and the orb gone. Plasmic broke the glass restraints and helped me off the platform.

"Ten minutes are up," said the two creatures, "Wait, Plasmic? Is this your new brother? You do remember what happened to your last brother, right?" Plasmic got in front of me.

"I do, but you shall not harm Plasmike," said Plasmic, "We were just about to leave anyway."

"You're not going anywhere," said the two creatures. One of the creatures flew towards Plasmic and tackled him. The other creature shot a bolt of orange lightning at me. I dodged the bolt and aimed my right arm at the creature. A bolt of blue lightning shot from my arm, but missed the creature. The creature dug its hand into the sand and pulled out a staff, made of glass. *I wonder...* I dug my right arm into the sand and thought of my favorite weapon. I felt something leave my arm and suddenly, something materialized into my hand.

I pulled my hand out of the sand and in my right hand was my favorite weapon, a sword. The creature flew towards me, and swung its staff at me. I heard the shatter of glass, as the staff broke against my arm. I swung my sword towards the creature, and sparks flew as the creature blocked my sword with the other half of its staff. I swung my sword a bit harder, and when the creature blocked, the impact of my sword shattered the creature's staff.

"Yield," I said, as I pointed my sword at the creature.

"I only yield when I've been beat," laughed the creature, as it punched my sword, causing it to shatter. The creature struck me with orange lightning, which caused me to fly backwards. I felt an intense pain in my right arm and my vision blurred.

"Micheal!" Plasmic screamed. When my vision cleared, I saw the creature flying towards me. Suddenly, my Aspergers kicked in, only instead of everything slowing down, everything stopped. *A glass ball to the face might work.* Everything slowly started to speed back up. I quickly got a handful of sand, sent some electricity to the sand, and threw it at the incoming creature. It was after I threw the glass ball when I saw something wrong. I didn't throw a glass ball, I threw a handful of sand.

The sand didn't do anything to the creature except stick to it. Then, right as the creature was about two inches in front of me, the grains of sand on the creature exploded. The shockwave knocked me to the ground and caused the creature to lose control of its flight. The creature crashed into the sand behind me. The other creature broke away from Plasmic and flew to the crash-landed creature. Plasmic got up and flew to me.

"Time to go," said Plasmic as he helped me up. Plasmic and I ran until we were back at the hut.

"Now that we're safe, you need to tell me what you just did back there," said Plasmic.

"Not until you tell what you did with the Orb of Conduct," I said.

"What I did was keep you from frying your bones every time you used your powers by fusing copper, aluminum, zinc, silver, and gold to them. It also fused high amounts of selenium into your skin, allowing better absorption of electricity," said Plasmic, "Now, tell me how you did what you did."

"I don't know, I just charged the sand," I said.

"You didn't charge the sand, you turned the grains of sand into thunder-balls," said Plasmic, "So tell me, how did you do that?"

"I already told you, I don't know," I said.

"So you really don't know?" Plasmic asked.

"No," I said.

"How curious, I don't know how you're able to create thunder-balls, because not even the most powerful electri can do that," Plasmic said, "Only electrets have that ability. Do you think you can do it again?"

"I can try," I said. I took off one of my shoes. Plasmic looked at me with curiosity, as I poured some sand out of my shoe and into my hand. I focused on sending electricity to the sand and imagined the sand becoming charged. Soon, the sand began to glow blue.

"That didn't happen last time," I said, with a mixture of curiosity and fear.

"Were you trying to create thunder-balls last time?" Plasmic asked.

"No," I said.

"That's probably why that's happening," Plasmic said, "Although, you probably shouldn't continue to hold them." I realized what he meant and quickly threw the thunder-balls up into the air. Nothing happened. The thunder-balls hit the ground, but still nothing happened. *Boom.* All the thunder-balls exploded, which startled both of us. *Interesting, they only explode when I want them to.*

"So, what are thunder-balls?" I asked.

"I'm not sure, some thunder-balls emit high levels of heat when they explode, while others emit powerful shockwaves. There are those who are a mixture of the two, and those that simply go boom," Plasmic answered, "Interestingly enough, some can be created out of thin air."

"How do you know so much about thunder-balls if electri can't create them?" I asked.

"Because I have a pet electret," Plasmic answered, "Wait a second, I just thought of something: what if you had an electret as a pet?"

"I don't know, how would my parents react? What would I feed it? How do electrets act? Are they destructive?" I asked.

"Keveal will explain everything to your parents, electrets eat the thunder-balls they create, they are as hyper as lightning, and not really if you train them, which is very simple," Plasmic said, "Trust me, you getting an electret will really help better your technique on creating thunder-balls."

"Okay, let's do it," I said. Plasmic smiled and took me to a heavily wooded area. "Where are we?"

"We're in the center of the electrets' main habitat," said Plasmic, as he put his hand up and made plasma dance from finger to finger. Soon, we heard what sounded like a ferret, only more electrical, behind us.

Plasmic lowered his hand and stopped the plasma. Plasmic and I turned around and saw a creature that resembled a ferret, only it was blue and yellow.

"Make some thunder-balls," said Plasmic. I made a few thunder-balls from the sand in my shoe and the ferret-like creature looked at me with curiosity. I lowered the thunder-balls, and the creature cautiously approached. The creature took the thunder-balls and ate them. *So that's an electret.* After the electret ate all the thunder-balls, it stood on its hind legs and looked eagerly at me.

I made more thunder-balls and gave them to the electret. Once the electret finished its snack, it ran towards my left leg. As soon as it got to my leg, it proceeded to climb up and get on my shoulders, generating sparks as it did. After it got on my shoulders, it sniffed my nose, gave it a quick lick, and went to my right shoulder.

"I think he likes you," said Plasmic, "What are you going to name him?"

"Uhh," I said as I looked at the electret, who started to generate sparks, "How about Sparks?"

"I think that's a good name," said Plasmic, "Time to head back."

"Oh yeah, we never completed the training," I said.

"No, we're done with today's training, what we need to do is rest," said Plasmic.

"But we only did two lessons," I said.

"We also fought two protos," said Plasmic, "Now, follow me." With Sparks on my shoulder, I followed Plasmic back to the building I awoke in. Plasmic led me to a room with a bed, gave me a black shirt, wished me "good dreams", and left. I sat down on the bed, holding the shirt Plasmic gave me, when I heard a knock on the door. Sparks jumped to the bed when I got up. I walked to the door and opened it to see Keveal-Chard on the other side.

"So how was your first day on Planet Electro?" he asked.

"A little fast, but pretty good," I answered.

"I'm glad you've enjoyed it, how have you adjusted to your 'gift'?" he asked.

"Pretty well," I said.

"That's good," he said, "how's your electret, Sparks?" I turned around, and saw Sparks sleeping on the pillow.

"Asleep," I said as I turned back to Keveal-Chard.

"Ha-ha, well, I better let you rest. Oh, before I forget, if you try on that electro armor, be sure to take off your bandages first," he said as he left. I walked back to the bed and sat down, staring at the black shirt. *How is this shirt armor?* I decided to try it on, so I took off my shirt and bandages. When I put the black shirt on, it stuck to me like a sock does to a shirt when they're fresh out of a dryer. Suddenly, I felt something stick from my hip down to my ankles, similar to the way the shirt stuck to my upper body.

I took my shoes and socks off, and saw the same material as the shirt stuck on my ankles. Though the electro armor was a little tight, it was soft as silk and very comfortable. I took off my jeans and climbed in bed. Sparks got up and got on my chest where he fell asleep a few seconds later. I soon fell asleep, and had an odd dream.

In my dream, I saw frids and electri battling giant scorpions. The dream shifted a little, and I suddenly saw myself and a giant tarantula fighting a single giant scorpion. The dream shifted again, and I saw the scorpion lunge towards my dream-self. The scorpion raised its stinger, and lunged it at my dream-self. But before the stinger hit my dream-self, the tarantula knocked me out of the way. I heard my dream-self scream "NOOoo!" as the tarantula got stabbed by the scorpion's stinger.

The dream shifted one last time, and I saw myself in front of the tarantula with tears streaming down my eyes. The tarantula's legs began to curl up. My dream-self quickly reached into my/his pocket, pulled out a strange metallic rod, and pointed it at the tarantula. Suddenly, a red beam, similar to the one that hit Alex, shot out of the rod and hit the tarantula. There was a bright flash, and the face of a beautiful blonde girl appeared. After the girl's face appeared, I woke up.

Chapter 3

When I woke up, I saw Plasmic, Keveal, and a frid standing next to my bed. None of them said anything, so I decided to get up. As soon as I stood up, my head began to hurt and I immediately felt light headed. I tried to keep standing, but my head kept hurting more and more. I fell back onto the bed. I put my right hand on my head, and it felt like my head was on fire. I put my left hand on the bed to push myself up, and noticed that where I put my hand was pretty damp.

"What's going on?" I asked weakly. Keveal, the frid, and Plasmic didn't say anything. They would just look at me, then at each other, then back at me.

"We don't know," Plasmic said finally, as he got closer to my bed, "Last night, you started screaming and shooting lightning everywhere. When we finally calmed you down, you had nearly used all of your electric supply, and you were burning up." I looked at my right arm to see my 'scars' barely glowing. I tried to get back up, but Plasmic stopped me.

"You need to rest and let your body naturally replenish your electric supply," said Plasmic.

"Okay, but could I at least get something to drink?" I asked. Plasmic nodded and left the room. When he came back, he had a glass cup filled with a blue liquid. Plasmic gave me the glass. I took a small sip, then quickly drank all the liquid, which tasted like blue raspberry. The drink completely quenched my thirst, and within a few minutes, my headache was gone. I immediately felt better, and tried to get up again. Plasmic stopped me, and gestured towards my right arm. I looked at my right arm to see the 'scars' still barely glowing.

"Until your electric supply is restored, you're going to rest," Plasmic.

"The best way for me to rest would probably be sleeping, however, due to some sort of mental tick, I can't go to sleep if I'm being watched," I said.

"Not a problem," said Plasmic, as he leaned closer to me and touched my forehead. As soon as he touched my forehead, I fainted and saw the girl's face again. She looked to be around fifteen. Her face faded away after a few minutes, and I woke up. After waking up, I looked at my right arm to see my 'scars' brightly glowing.

"*Feel better?*" Keveal asked.

"Much," I said, as I got up. I looked behind me, and Sparks fast asleep.

"*Good, Plasmic is waiting outside to continue your training,*" he said, "*That reminds me, Plasmic told me to tell you to keep your electro armor on and to keep your shoes off.*" Keveal led me to Plasmic, then left to go consult with an elder.

"Now that you're here, we can begin lesson three," Plasmic said happily.

"You seem happy," I said.

"I am," said Plasmic, "Now, your electro armor is very important, especially for this and further lessons. It will help with battle, as it helps you generate electricity faster and if used properly, can make your attacks more powerful. I've set up a few targets for you to hit using your powers, in seven minutes."

"That doesn't sound too hard, how many targets are there?" I asked.

Plasmic smiled and said "There are seventy targets. Lesson three: when you need to find what is lost within a certain time, the path of lightning may quicken your journey. With your electro armor, you can safely morph into an electrical form. In this form, you will be able to literally be lightning fast.

To enter this form, focus on being one with the electricity around you." I focused and a second later, my vision switched to my electro sight. My body began to fill with energy. I looked at my hands, and was a little shocked to see them in a sort of electrical outline.

"So where are these targets?" I asked.

"Scattered across Planet Electro," Plasmic said.

"Wait, how am I supposed to find these targets? I don't even know what they look like," I said.

"You'll know them when you see them, for they are in seven groups of ten. Each group will be in the shape of a circle," Plasmic said.

"And how am I supposed find all these groups if I only have seven minutes?" I asked. Plasmic didn't say anything, but instead looked towards the clouds in the sky. *If I'm in an electrical form, perhaps I can travel along the clouds as lightning.* I looked towards the clouds and a half-second later, was in the clouds.

"You might not want to go that fast," I heard Plasmic say, "I'll come get you if time runs out. If you finish before time runs out, get to the ground and send lightning towards the sky. You have seven minutes starting now, good luck." I headed north, looking towards the ground, and quickly found my first group. *Down.* I landed as a lightning strike, hit all the targets, and flew back into the clouds.

Once I was in the clouds, I went west and found my second group. *Wait, if I can create a pulse of static electricity, could I create an explosion of electricity?* I sent some electricity to my right fist, and landed the same way I did before. Only this time, I punched the ground with my charged fist when I landed. There was a loud boom and my electro sight blurred. When my sight cleared, I was standing in a crater and all the targets in the group were eradicated. *Whoops, maybe I shouldn't do this to any of the other groups.*

I flew back into the clouds, and traveled south. I didn't find a group, so I decided to go south-east and found my third group. *Perhaps some ball lightning will work better.* I landed and imagined ten ball lightning orbs. In an instant, ten orbs of ball lightning were orbiting around me. I put my hands together and the orbs stopped. I quickly pulled my hands apart and the orbs flew into the targets. I closed my right fist, and the orbs flew back to me and began to orbit once more. I flew back into the clouds, with the orbs following me, and headed north-east.

I spotted my fourth group pretty quickly. *I could probably send the ball lightning down there and save time.* I twisted my right arm like I was screwing in a light bulb. Suddenly, the orbs began to increase their orbiting speed. I opened my right fist and the orbs spread apart. I sent my fist downward and the orbs flew towards the targets. After the orbs hit the targets, I brought my fist up and the orbs flew back into the clouds.

I went north-west and found my fifth group, surrounding the hut where Plasmic created the Orb of Conduct. I hit the targets with the ball lightning. *I wonder...* After I hit the targets, I headed towards the desert where I fought a proto. I found my sixth group surrounding the platform where Plasmic fused the Orb of Conduct into my bones. I quickly hit the targets, and headed towards the heavily wooded area where I found Sparks.

I quickly found my seventh and final group. I landed in the center of the group, whereas the ball lightning landed on each target. Once all the targets were hit, I put my right arm in the air and closed my fist tightly. The ball lightning got very close to my arm. I pointed my index finger toward the sky, the ball lightning struck the clouds as regular lightning spreading from cloud to cloud, and Plasmic arrived a second later.

"Done with only a minute left to spare, good job," said Plasmic.

"Thanks," I said.

"Now, follow me," said Plasmic as he flew up into the clouds. I followed him up into the clouds and he led me back to the spot Keveal took me to. This time, however, there was a huge boulder.

"That wasn't there before," I said once we landed.

"That's because I brought it here," said Plasmic, "For this next lesson, you can be in your original form. To switch back to your original form, all you have to do is think about it." I thought about it and a second later, I was back to my normal form.

"This is a little off topic, but important nonetheless," Plasmic started, "Never enter your electrical form unless you have your electro armor. The consequences of doing so can be fatal."

"Okay," I said.

"Now, back to the subject on hand, try to move this boulder," said Plasmic. I went up to the boulder and pushed as hard as I could, but failed to move it.

"Lesson four: no matter how impossible it may seem, you can move any obstacle if you set your mind to it. Surround the boulder with plasma and positively charge the boulder's core," said Plasmic, "This is what electri know as plasma-kinesis." I did what Plasmic said, then tried to lift the boulder using plasma-kinesis. It was hard and I was only able to lift it a foot off the ground. I struggled to keep the boulder in the air, but for some odd reason, the muscles in my arms, mainly my right arm, started to ache. I released the boulder, which hit the ground with a thud, and clutched my right arm.

"Are you okay?" Plasmic asked.

"Yeah, my right arm is aching, but I'll live," I said.

"Ha-ha, that's because plasma-kinesis requires muscle and mental strength with a dash of electrical powers," said Plasmic, "You should've seen Hercules when he used plasma-kinesis for the first time. He could barely lift his target two inches."

"I thought Hercules had the strength of a god," I said.

"Oh, he had the muscle, just not the mental strength," said Plasmic, "But it was the funniest thing I've ever seen. The face he was making as he struggled and the fact that he turned red made me and my brother laugh so hard that my brother had to pause the lesson so he could get it together."

"Is this the same brother the protos mentioned?" I asked.

"Onto the next lesson," Plasmic said, trying to change the subject.

"That didn't answer my question," I said.

"Yes, that was the same brother the protos mentioned, now can we please move on to the next lesson?" Plasmic asked, his voice cracking as he spoke, "Because talking about my deceased brother depresses me."

"Oh. I'm sorry to hear about your brother," I said sincerely.

"It's okay, you didn't know," said Plasmic, looking away.

"So, what's the next lesson about?" I asked, trying to change the subject.

"I think you'll like it," Plasmic said, his mood brighter, "Shoot a normal bolt of lightning at the boulder." I shot the boulder with lightning, but all it did was leave a black mark where the lightning struck it.

"Lesson five: there are times to attack and there times to charge… then attack," said Plasmic, "Charge your electro armor, then shoot the boulder again." I charged my electro armor and its sleeves began to lengthen until they reached my wrists. After that, blue plasma danced from my right wrist to my right shoulder. The same thing happened with my left wrist and shoulder, except it was yellow lightning instead of blue plasma. I looked at the boulder, aimed my right arm at it, and shot it with blue lightning. The boulder exploded with a loud bang, leaving a trail of smoke and small pebbles where it once stood. Any piece of the boulder that would've hit us was caught by Plasmic via plasma-kinesis.

"Good job," Plasmic said, as he released the rocks.

"Thanks" I said.

"Now that you're done with today's lessons, there's someone I'd like you to meet," said Plasmic, "Follow me." I followed Plasmic to a huge, old palace. The palace was as white as quartz and glowing fairly well. There were seven tall pillars in front of entrance, and as we got closer to the pillars, I noticed they had a lightning pattern carved into them. When we entered the palace, an electro, that looked like Plasmic but older, approached us.

"Welcome to the Palace of the Elders, my name is Nelb Yil," said the electro, "I am one of seven Elder Electri."

"My name is Plasmike," I said, as I extended my hand, "Pleasure to meet you."

"Pleasure to meet you too, now," Nelb said as he grabbed my hand for a second, then turned towards Plasmic, "Is something wrong, or are you here to talk?

"We're here to talk," Plasmic answered.

"Very well, follow me," Nelb said. Plasmic and I followed Nelb to a heptagonal room with a table in the middle. In the center of the table was a bowl of crystals. Nelb took a seat at the table and motioned us to do the same.

"So, what is it that you wish to talk about?" Nelb asked once Plasmic and I were seated.

"I think Plasmike might be the 'Prophesized One'," Plasmic said, grabbing my curiosity and Nelb's attention.

"Prophesized One?" I asked curiously.

"What evidence do you have to support this claim?" Nelb asked.

"The prophecy says that the Prophesized One will wield thunder-balls," Plasmic said.

"What prophecy?" I asked.

"You wield thunder-balls?" Nelb asked, as he turned to me.

"Yes," I answered, "But what's the prophecy?"

"I'll tell you later," Nelb said, "But first, prove to me that you can wield thunder-balls."

"Okay, but I might need some sand," I said, as I reached for my shoe.

"Nonsense, just use the air around you and do the same thing you'd do with sand," Nelb said.

"Uhh, okay," I said, nervously. I shot Plasmic with a look of concern, as I cupped my hands together and focused on charging the air inside. Nothing happened. I opened my hands, but didn't see anything.

"Try again," Nelb said, "But this time, pretend like you're feeding your electret, Sparks."

"That's a bit creepy… how'd you know about Sparks?" I asked, nervously.

"Sorry if I creeped you out. I knew because I shook your hand," Nelb explained, "You see, with electri and protos, physical contact is, well, it's like what humans do when they connect a flash drive to a computer. My comparison is another example of this, as I used your memories and knowledge to help you understand this concept."

"Good to know," I said, "But it's still creepy." I cleared my mind, then imagined myself about to feed Sparks. I felt thunder-balls materialize inside my hands a few seconds later. I opened my hands and showed the thunder-balls to Nelb. Everyone jumped to their feet as something burst into the room and made a beeline for the thunder-balls in my hand. It was Sparks. We all sat back down and continued our conversation.

"Interesting, what other evidence do you have?" Nelb asked as he turned to Plasmic.

"He survived the bonding of the Orb of Conduct," Plasmic said.

"Wait, what do you mean I survived?" I asked.

"Hmm, your evidence is valid," Nelb said as he grabbed a crystal out of the bowl, "Plasmike, hold this." Nelb gave me the crystal. As soon as the crystal touched my skin, its edges began to glow golden yellow and a golden, wavy cross formed inside of it. Suddenly, I felt tons of energy flow from the crystal to my body.

"I always thought the arrival of the Prophesized One would be long after my time had passed, please keep that mimic crystal as a gift," Nelb said as he turned to Plasmic, "And Plasmic…"

"Yeah, Dad?" Plasmic replied.

"Train him well," Nelb said, then turned back to me with a blank expression,

"In futurity, I view a painful scene. Three friends you'll see, two will see the grave. The third to thieves of life, the key to never die. The thieves who seek the key, destroy all in their way. Generations old, become them hate and cold. If thieves take the key, she'll not see light of day. Seeking Lyca's eternity, the thieves forfeit their purity."

"If them you face, time against you'll race. Sparing them is vain, mercy will you not receive. Encountering Siphe, you'll fight for your life. To seal their fate, from them keep the key. Should it thieves steal, stronger will they be. For Lyca's Vine they came, for immortality. In you must awake, for her bonds to break. In you *Hogo Seishin* stays, in you the spirit sleeps. The spirit of legend, may bring to Siphe an end."

"I'm sorry," Nelb said, his expression back to normal, "I wasn't expecting a vision today. I hope I didn't creep you out. Farewell, and don't forget what was foretold." Plasmic and I said "bye" to Nelb, and left the Palace of the Elders.

"What do we do now?" I asked.

"Well, your final lessons aren't due 'til tomorrow, and the day's not over yet," Plasmic started, "I guess we could play some Ping-Pong."

"Ping-Pong?" I laughed, "I thought that was an Earth thing."

"It started on Earth," Plasmic said, "But a few years ago, while exploring Earth to study its life forms, Keveal and I came across some people playing Ping-Pong. Using Keveal's telepathic abilities, we approached them as humans and asked what they were doing. They told us, then taught us how to play. Upon our return to Planet Electro, Keveal taught the frids how to play, while I taught the electri. It's been played on Planet Electro ever since."

"Cool," I said, "let's do it."

"Alright, follow me," Plasmic said. I followed Plasmic to a two story building.

"Welcome to my home," Plasmic said as we entered the building, "The Ping-Pong table is this way." Plasmic led me to the Ping-Pong table, handed me a paddle, and went to his side of the table.

"First to five?" Plasmic asked.

"Sure," I said. Plasmic served the ball, but when I tried to return it, it bounced on my side. Plasmic served again, and the same thing happened. *He's spinning it.* Plasmic served it for the third time, but this time, I angled my paddle up as I returned the ball. The ball bounced of my paddle and just missed the net as it landed on Plasmic's side. My success, however, was short-lived, because right after the ball bounced on Plasmic's side, Plasmic spiked the ball and scored his third point.

I prepared for the spin on Plasmic's fourth serve, but Plasmic never spun the ball. The ball flew out of bounds, awarding Plasmic his fourth point. Since it was game point, I got to serve. Using a technique a friend taught me, I spun the ball on my serve. Plasmic tried to return the ball, but failed. I didn't spin the ball on my second serve. Plasmic did a nice return and we volleyed until Plasmic hit the ball a little high. I took my chance and spiked it, scoring my second point.

I caught up to Plasmic after my third and fourth serve. Because we were tied on game point, we played until one of us was two points ahead. Plasmic soon beat me eighteen to sixteen.

"That was fun," Plasmic said after Ping-Pong ended, "But now you should probably get some sleep, you'll need it for tomorrow."

"Alright," I said. Plasmic led me back to the building I woke up in.

"Whoops, I almost forgot," Plasmic said as he touched my right arm, causing the sleeves on the electro armor to retract, "That's better, good dreams." After saying "good night", I went to my room, where Sparks jumped from my shoulder to the bed and laid on my pillow. I picked Sparks up, got in bed, and went to sleep.

Chapter 4: Plasmic

Plasmic, after confirming Plasmike was asleep, quickly flew to the residence of Keveal-Chard. He had a few questions to ask, especially about something called the Hogo Seishin. Plasmic had heard of it many times, in fact, it's in almost every frid prophecy. But never had it appeared in an electro or proto prophecy.

"What's the Hogo Seishin?" Plasmic asked as Keveal greeted him.

"It's an ancient secret, only the Elders know," Keveal said to his old friend, "All I can say for sure is that it's a legendary spirit. But what brings you to this question?"

"The Elder Electro, Nelb Yil, foretold it was asleep in within Plasmike," Plasmic said, "But he has never even heard of it, nor has it appeared in any prior visions foretold by Elder Electri or the Proto Elder, yet it is mentioned and referenced in many frid prophecies."

"I'm afraid I cannot give you an explanation, I'm just as confused as you are," Keveal said, rubbing his chin, "Tomorrow, one or two hours before you give the last two lessons, I will take Micheal to the Elders. Perhaps they can answer this conundrum. I'll take care of the rest, you should go to your home and get some sleep."

Plasmic, knowing he had to prepare for tomorrow's lessons, wished his friend "good dreams" and went to his home.

Chapter 5: Micheal

I awoke to the sound of someone knocking on my door. I gently moved Sparks off my chest, and got up to check the door. I opened the door to see Keveal, accompanied by a frid.

"What's going on?" I asked, yawning.

"The Elders wish to speak to you," Keveal said.

"Okay," I said, "Why?" I suddenly felt something land on my back and rise to my shoulders. I looked to my left shoulder and saw Sparks looking straight ahead.

"Just a routine checkup," Keveal answered, "All half-brothers do this. Ready?"

"I guess," I said. I followed Keveal outside to a castle-like building, surrounded by water. As we got closer, I noticed lots of frids swimming in the water and flying around the building. Once inside, Keveal led me to a large room, with four throne-like chairs at the end. Sitting in the chairs were old frids.

"Step forward, young one," said a frid's deep voice. I approached the frids.

"We are the Elder Frids of Enilas," said the frid, "Welcome."

"Um, thanks," I said.

"We wish to ask you some questions, as is customary," said another frid, *"Please answer them honestly."* The frids got up and walked towards me.

"Have you been able to use your gift without difficulties?" asked the first frid as the frid got closer to me.

"Well, I haven't really had a problem controlling my powers," I answered.

"Next question, have you been learning how appropriately use your gift?" the frid asked.

"Yeah, Plasmic's a good teacher," I said.

"Next question, have you had any weird or odd dreams?" the frid asked, catching me off guard.

"Yeah, but what does that have to with anything?" I asked, thinking about the dream I had my first night, "How would that affect my powers?"

"It's just a control question, though we've never had someone answer yes," the frid said, "Final question, would you like to have the power of telepathy?"

"Uh, sure, I guess," I said, completely confused.

"Hold out your hand," said the frid, as they approached me.

I put out my hand, and the frid dropped a feather into it. As soon as the feather touched my hand, I fell to my knees and experienced intense pain in my right arm. Suddenly, I saw a man with a villainous smile standing in front of me. I screamed as the pain moved to my head. I realized that the feather was what caused this and quickly dropped it.

The pain stopped once the feather left my hand. I slowly rose to my feet and looked angrily at the frid who gave me the feather.

"Why'd you give me that?!?" I asked lividly.

"We didn't think that would happen," said the frid, "It was supposed to give you the ability to communicate telepathically, not allow you to see visions."

"This is interesting," said another frid, *"The ability to see visions correlates to the prophecy of the Protector."*

"Perhaps the Hogo Seishin sleeps within you after all," said a third frid, *"But is it really able to defeat thieves of life?"*

"Siphe," I said to myself, which got all the frids', including Keveal's, attention.

"How do you know of Siphe?" Keveal asked.

"From the vision I got from the Elder Electro Nelb Yil," I said.

"You have great power within you," said the first frid as a familiar metallic rod floated towards him, *"But you are not ready to face Siphe. Here, take this. Don't worry, this won't do what the feather did."* The frid gave me the rod and I put it in my pocket.

"What does this do?" I asked.

"It has more functions than we can mention," said the frid, *"This device can help turn a battle in your favor."*

"Time to go," Keveal said. Keveal led me out of the building, and I followed him to Plasmic.

"Ready for your final two lessons?" Plasmic asked.

"Yep," I said.

"Good," Plasmic said, "Follow me." I followed Plasmic to two boulders.

"Put two holes in one of these boulders using only your eyes," said Plasmic.

"How?" I asked.

"Lesson six: sometimes to solve a problem, you'll need *laser* focus, literally," Plasmic said, "Use your eyes as the lens, and then supply them with plasma. Don't forget to charge the plasma." I focused plasma into my eyes, and looked at one of the boulders. I charged the plasma and my vision tinted blue, as lasers shot from my eyes and hit the boulder. The boulder smoked for a few seconds. I stopped charging the plasma, and my vision returned to normal.

"Excellent," Plasmic said looking at the two holes in the boulder, "Onto the next lesson. Punch the other boulder." I punched the hole less boulder, which caused some small pieces to break off.

"Good," Plasmic said, "But can you punch a hole into it? Without breaking anymore pieces off?"

"I'm not sure," I said.

"Lesson seven: sometimes, the situation may call for precise actions instead of brute force," Plasmic said, "Send electrical currents through the skin on your hand. Then, once your skin is hot enough, punch the boulder." I sent electrical currents through the skin of my right hand. My skin was red hot within a few seconds, and white hot within a minute. I punched the boulder again, and left a hole the size of my fist, without breaking off any pieces. After that, I shut off the electrical currents in my skin.

"Bravo!" Plasmic said, "That's the last of your lessons, which means it's almost time for you to leave."

"I guess that means we should return to Keveal," I said.

"Yep, but not yet," Plasmic said, "I need to share some important information with you. First, these seven lessons that I gave you are just the basics, most half-brothers get the hang of them on their first try, like you did, so don't get cocky. Second, while your powers do grant you full control over the nervous system, messing with it can have terrible consequences, so tread lightly. Third, your electro armor can take the form of any type of clothing you choose. Fourth, you can decide whether or not your electrical supply glows. And finally, to send you off, please shake my hand." Plasmic extended his right hand and caused white lightning to dance from finger to finger. I grabbed his hand, but never got to shake it. My right arm became stiff for two seconds, then loosened after Plasmic let go.

"Are you ever going to actually shake my hand?" I asked. Suddenly, my right hand shook for a second, then stopped.

"I just did," Plasmic laughed.

"That's not what I meant," I said, "Why'd you ask me to shake your hand anyway?"

"So I could give you a gift," Plasmic said, "The gift of Light, now come on, Keveal is waiting." Plasmic led me back to Keveal, who had a way back to Earth. A wormhole.

"Ready?" Keveal asked.

"Yep," I answered.

"Good, go," Plasmic said as he pushed Sparks and me into the wormhole.

Chapter 6

I was back in my woods a second later, and heard a howl. *Alex!* I ran back to the tree Alex climbed to find it surrounded by leaf wolves.

"Aww, the puppies don't know how to climb trees," I said mockingly.

"Well, isn't this a surprise," said a leaf wolf, "Kill him." One of the leaf wolves ran towards me. I aimed my right arm at the leaf wolf and shot it with lightning, causing it to fly backwards.

"Silly little puppy," I laughed.

"I said KILL HIM!" said the first leaf wolf. Two more leaf wolves ran toward me, but turned to ash as I shot them using my laser sight.

"Look, no hands," I said, "And for my final trick, I'm going to make the leaf wolves disappear." I charged my right fist, and ran at the leaf wolves. I leaped into the air, and punched the ground as I landed next to the leaf wolves. With a loud boom and a snap, the leaf wolves were eradicated, and the tree was falling over....with Alex still on it.

Using plasma kinesis, I caught the tree, and slowly lowered it to the ground. Once it was safe, Alex stepped onto the ground and walked towards me.

"P-please don't d-do that again," Alex said.

"I'll try not to," I said, "Which way to that guy you were talking to earlier?" Alex pointed straight behind me. I turned around and ran until I saw the man fighting Logan. *I could probably hack into the man's brain and find out when and where the Wilsons will be at.* I shut off the nerves in the man's eyes and ears, and ran at him. I tackled him and touched a finger to his temple. I was able to get in his mind and search for the information I needed in a few seconds. I found it a few seconds later. I got off of the man and ran to Logan.

"Time to run," I said.

"What's that on your shoulder?" Logan asked.

"I'll tell you later, now run," I said, "I'll meet you back at the house." I turned towards the man, while Logan ran to the house. I imagined the electro armor becoming a ninja suit, and a second later, the electro armor became a ninja suit. With my face masked, I turned the man's nerves back on. He got up and looked at me.

"Your plan will fail," I said.

"You think so?" the man laughed.

"Yep, because I'm going to foil it," I said as I shot lightning in front of his feet.

"How do you plan on doing that?" the man asked.

"You'll see how in three days," I said as Sparks and I entered our electrical forms and flew to the house.

We changed back to our original forms as we landed in the driveway, and entered the house through the front door. Not wanting to startle my parents, I quickly switched the electro armor back to normal and entered the living room.

"The frog-thing is real," Logan said as I entered the living room, "Sorry, frid." My parents and Logan were sitting on the couch, whereas Keveal and Plasmic sat on the fireplace.

"Now that he's here, can you please tell us what's going on?" my dad asked Keveal and Plasmic.

"Perhaps it'd be best if the three of us gave an explanation," Keveal said.

"I'll start," I said. I told my parents everything that had happened from entering the woods to waking up on Planet Electro. Then

Plasmic explained everything that had happened the three days I was on Planet Electro. Once Plasmic finished, Keveal stared at my parents.

"The powers MUST be kept secret, only family members can know," Keveal finally said. Keveal and Plasmic got up, said "farewell", and left.

Chapter 7

School was closed the next day due to snow, so I slept until 9:16 am. After breakfast, I went into the woods to find Alex. I needed to find out what he knew about the plan. After an hour of searching without finding, I headed back to the house. On my way to the house, I spotted a black-t and though it wasn't Alex, I knew I could get the information I needed. Doing the same thing I did to the man, I hacked into the black-t's brain and acquired the information I needed: how the black-ts planned on getting the car to crash.

With the information acquired, I decided to head back to the house to come up with a counterplan. Along the way, I had a gut feeling that I was being spied on. *Better to be safe than sorry.* I turned the electro armor back into its ninja variant and switched to my electro sight. I didn't create a pulse, but instead searched for the electricity of a nervous system. *There, sixteen feet up in the trees.* I shot a bolt of lightning at the branch holding the spy.

With a snap, the branch fell taking the spy with it. I approached the spy to find out why I was being followed when I felt the electricity of another nervous system behind me. I turned around to see another spy running at me. I charged the electro armor, and both spies gasped. I switched back to my human vision to see that the two spies were dressed as ninjas but no taller than me.

"Who are you and why were you spying on me?" I asked.

"We weren't spying on you, we were just following you without you knowing about it," said a familiar voice.

"Which is spying, *Wesley*," I said as I discharged the electro armor. (Wesley is a friend of mine who is a year older than Logan, but is in my grade. He comes from a rich family, and has a sister, named Mindy, who is as old as Logan.)

"See, I told you he'd recognize you," said Mindy the other spy, as she took off her ninja mask.

"Yes you did, would you like a medal?" Wesley asked mockingly, as he took off his mask, "You can take off the mask, Micheal. We saw you put it on."

"Why are you two here?" I asked as I changed the electro armor into a long-sleeved variation of itself with a hoodie.

"I wanted to see if I was right about you being chosen," Wesley said, "Looks like I was, but don't worry, your secret's safe with us."

"So you were spying on me yesterday?" I asked.

"Yes," Wesley said, "Because I had to. Our *ninjitsu* instructor told us to follow a friend for a week without the friend knowing. A friend of mine tried doing it to me, but I caught him because he was a little too noisy."

"Speaking of which, we better start heading back," Mindy said, "Our next lesson will start soon and we don't want to be late."

"You have a ninjitsu lesson on a snow day?" I asked, "I thought everything was closed due to snow."

"The dojo's closed, but my dad is the instructor," Wesley said, "I'll see you later." Wesley and Mindy left, and I headed back to the house.

Once I got to the house, I gathered the family chess set and a box of Legos, and went upstairs to my room. Sparks greeted me as I entered by climbing to my shoulders and licking my nose. I walked to the center of my room, set the chess set and Legos on the floor, and yelled for Logan. Once Logan entered the room and sat down, I emptied the box of Legos and collected the white king and queen, one of the white bishops, one of the white rooks, the black king, and all of the black pawns from the chess set.

I surrounded all the chess pieces and Legos with plasma and charged their cores. Using plasma-kinesis, I quickly made a Lego house and placed the white king, queen, and bishop next to it. I then made some Lego trees, a Lego car, and a Lego road. I placed the trees on both sides of the road to represent the location of the future car wreck. I placed the car on the road, and the white rook and black pawns along the trees.

"Remember the man from the woods?" I asked.

"Yeah, why?" Logan asked.

"Remember what he said?" I asked.

"Yeah, he was telling the black-t to cause a car wreck," Logan said, "And that he was going to stall some godparents while a comrade kidnaps the girl from the wreck at the hospital."

"Do you know who the godparents are?" I asked.

"I don't think so," Logan said curiously.

"They're Mom and Dad," I said, "And yesterday, when I tackled the man and hacked into his brain, I found out that he knew who we were, and how he planned on stalling Mom and Dad. He's going to use a genetically mutated creature called Daizer."

"Daizer?" Logan asked.

"A creature of pure malice," I explained, "It's about six feet tall and covered in fur. It's very strong, very resilient, and very loud."

"We have to tell Mom and Dad about this," Logan said as he abruptly got up and headed towards the door.

"No," I said as I stopped him, "At least, not yet. If they find out now, they'll mess up my counterplan."

"Counterplan?" Logan asked, "You mean you have a way to defeat the Daizer?"

"Yep," I said as I pointed to the house, "At 1:00 pm this Sunday, the Daizer will be at the house. What I need you-"

"Me?" Logan interrupted, "You're not going to fight it?"

"I'll be preventing the car from crashing at that time," I said, "Now, what I need you to do is keep it away from Mom and Dad's cars, but mainly away from Mom and Dad."

"Yep, because a six foot beast is going to listen to a ten year old," Logan said sarcastically, "Are you really going to leave Mom, Dad, and me alone to fight this thing?"

"I never said I was going to leave you alone," I said with a smile.

"What do you mean?" Logan asked.

"I mean that when I saw the Daizer in the man's mind, I knew I had to find out everything the man knew about it," I said.

"What are you trying to say?" Logan asked curiously.

"I'm trying to say that the man created the Daizer using stolen frid technology," I said as I grabbed the metallic rod the frids gave me, "And I know how he did it."

"So you're going to create a Daizer?" Logan asked.

"No, something better than a Daizer," I said, "Go get Dylan." (Dylan is my grandmother's insane, energetic Boston terrier who I was dog sitting for two weeks.)

"Okay," Logan said as he left, a little confused. While Logan was gone, I gave the rod some power. It started to glow, and I saw all its functions. **To use a function, will it to happen on selected target.**

To use multiple functions at once, charge device and will desired functions to happen. Logan returned with Dylan and sat down. I aimed the rod at Dylan, charged it, and chose five functions: invulnerate; rapid, reversible metamorphose; strengthen; key code; and cloneable. The rod made a buzzing sound and shot Dylan with a bright orange beam of light.

"Is that it?" Logan asked.

"You might want to put Dylan down," I said. Logan put Dylan down and scooted back.

"Now what?" Logan asked.

"Dylan, *Stronghold*," I said. Suddenly, Dylan rapidly metamorphosed into a six foot, muscular hulk.

"Nice job, you just mutated Gran's dog into a monster," Logan said.

"Did I?" I said with a smile, "Dylan, *Revert*." Dylan reverted back to her Boston terrier form as quickly as she had metamorphosed.

"Impressive," Logan said, "But what makes Dylan different from the Daizer?"

"The Daizer only has one form," I said, "Dylan has two: an invulnerable form and a powerful form."

"Is there anything else I should know?" Logan asked.

"Make sure you have something to cover your ears when you see the Daizer," I said, "And remember the keyword *intimidate*."

"Okay," Logan said, "Hey, after you complete your counterplan, do you want to have a snowball fight?"

"Yeah, sounds like fun," I said as I turned to the Lego car.

"Alright, come downstairs when you're finished," Logan said as he got up and left. Once Logan was gone, I began working on my plan to prevent the car wreck. I quickly thought up a plan a few seconds later. It was simple, the black-ts were going to tie a wire to two trees and let the car run into it. All I'd have to do is break the wire. Only one problem: Lucius, a member of Siphe would be there to overlook everything. Remembering what Nelb and the elder frid said, I figured I'd sneak past him. After I finished creating my counterplan, I grabbed Dylan and Sparks, and headed downstairs. I met up with Logan and we went outside.

"Why do you have Dylan and that thing?" Logan asked once we were outside.

"First off, he's not a thing, he's an electret. Secondly, his name is Sparks. Thirdly, I doubt he's ever seen snow on Planet Electro, so I wanted to see how he would react to it," I said as I put Sparks on the snow. The snow was still soft and just a little taller than Sparks, so Sparks fell through the snow as soon as I let go of him. Sparks inspected the snow for a few seconds and tried to tunnel through it, but didn't succeed because the snow was too soft.

"Sorry Sparks, you'll have to wait 'til tomorrow if you want to tunnel," I said. Sparks shook the snow off his head, sniffed around for a few seconds then started to hop around from one spot to another, falling through the snow as he did. Logan and I laughed as Sparks continuously jumped and disappeared into the snow.

"I think he likes it," Logan said, "But what about Dylan? Why is she here?"

"For the snowball fight," I said as put Dylan down, "Dylan, *Duo*." I noticed a single hair fall off Dylan, and from that single hair grew a nearly identical, orange tinted clone.

"This'll be interesting," Logan said with a smile.

"Yep," I said, "Dylans, *Stronghold*." Both Dylans metamorphosed. By hacking into their brains, I taught them how to do a snowball fight.

"It's us versus the Dylans," I said, "Get to your starting positions, the snowball fight will commence in five minutes." Logan and I rushed to our starting positions, and quickly started working on making a fort. The Dylans did the same.

After five minutes, I had my half of the fort high enough to duck under. I glanced over at Logan's half to see that it was not only taller, but wider and thicker than my half. Logan also had a pyramid of snowballs already made. The strange thing was that the snow around him looked almost untouched.

"How'd you make all of that without using any snow?" I asked.

"It's simple, I just-DUCK!!" Logan exclaimed. I ducked and a snowball flew over me. I grabbed a snowball from Logan's pyramid and threw it at the Dylans. I looked back at Logan's half to find the snow around him seemed to have been used to make his half and the snowballs. *Strange*.

"Incoming snowballs," Logan said, "Take cover." Logan and I took cover as a barrage of snowballs flew past us. I quickly made some snowballs while Logan kept the fort intact. Once the barrage ended, Logan and I threw all of our snowballs at the Dylans. A few of the snowballs hit the Dylans, so they built their fort a little higher.

"Now how are we supposed to get them?" Logan asked.

"Like this," I said as I positively charged the cores of two snowballs. I threw the two snowballs at both sides of the Dylans' fort. Once the snowballs were past the fort, I used plasma-kinesis to bring the snowballs towards each other and hit the Dylans. With a yelp, both Dylans jumped a few feet in the air. The Dylans retaliated by sending barrage after barrage of snowballs. Logan and I soon had no choice but to surrender.

After the snowball fight, I *reverted* both Dylans, got Sparks, and headed inside for a late lunch. Once lunch was over, I went upstairs and got a backpack. I headed back downstairs and made seven roast beef sandwiches. I put the sandwiches into sandwich bags, then the sandwich bags into a gallon bag with the inside lined with paper towels, and finally, the gallon bag into another gallon bag that would later be filled with snow.

I put the gallon bag into the backpack and retrieved nine bottled waters. After I put the waters into the backpack, I grabbed a blanket and put it into the backpack. *The mimic crystal may come in handy if something goes wrong.* I went upstairs to my room and grabbed the mimic crystal. While I was in my room, I decided go through my counterplan one more time. After I finished going through my counterplan, I went downstairs to get a wire cutter.

"What are you doing?" my dad asked as went towards the tool room.

"Getting some supplies," I answered.

"Supplies for what?" my dad asked.

"Supplies for camping tonight and tomorrow night in the woods," I said.

"Why do you want to camp in the woods?" my dad asked.

"For the fun of it," I lied.

"Well, put a coat on," my dad said "And make sure to back before 3:00 pm this Sunday, I have some friends coming over and I would like you to meet them." My dad left and I went into the tool room and acquired the wire cutter. I put the wire cutter into the backpack and went to the closet to get a coat. Once I had the coat on and the backpack on my back, I grabbed Sparks and the Dylan clone and headed down into the woods. Based on the information I got from the black-t and the man, it would take me the rest of the day and all day tomorrow to get to the road the Wilsons will be driving on.

Once I entered the woods, I stopped and filled the gallon bag containing the other gallon bag with snow. After I put the gallon bag back into the backpack, I walked toward my destination with the Dylan clone and Sparks following close behind. As we were walking, the temperature began to drop. Even with the coat and electro armor on, I began feeling cold. To keep myself from suffering hypothermia, I sent small electrical currents through my bones.

Sparks apparently got tired of being cold because an hour after I heated my bones, he ran up my leg and into an interior coat pocket. I looked at the Dylan clone and saw her shivering. *I might be able to keep her warm if I put her in my coat.* I picked the Dylan clone up, put her in my coat, and continued walking.

I began to get hungry at 6:00 pm, so I stopped near a tree and ate for about ten minutes, and fed Sparks and the Dylan clone five minutes later. Once the three of us were fed and Sparks and the Dylan clone was back in my coat, I continued my walk until it got dark forty five minutes later. Once it got dark, I got the blanket out of the backpack and laid against a tree. I fell asleep twenty two minutes later.

Chapter 8

I woke up at around 8:26 am, put the blanket into the backpack, got a sandwich, and made a few thunder-balls for Sparks. Once the three of us finished breakfast and everyone was in my coat, I continued my walk. For some odd reason, Sparks started to make a clicking noise at around 10:06 am. The Dylan clone began to growl fifty nine minutes later. *What's going on?*

"I've never been known for my patience," said a voice from behind me. I quickly switched the electro armor to its ninja suit variant and turned around to see the man from two days ago. Standing next to him was a Daizer.

"So surrender now, and maybe I let you live," said the man.

"And if I refuse?" I asked.

"I'll unleash the Daizer on you," the man said with a malicious smile.

"Oh no, not the Daizer," I said sarcastically.

"I'm serious," the man said.

"Gasp, you hear that Sparks? He's serious," I said, barely keeping a straight face, "Red Rover, Red Rover, send the Daizer right over."

"That's it, don't say I didn't warn you," the man said, "Any last words?"

"Just one," I said as I pulled the Dylan clone out of my coat and put her in front of me, "*Stronghold.*" The Dylan clone metamorphosed into her powerful form, a six foot, muscular hulk.

"You think this thing will be able to defeat the Daizer?" the man laughed, "*Daze.*" The Daizer screeched, making me dazed for a few seconds. The Dylan clone, however, didn't even flinch.

"Not bad," I said, "Watch this, *Intimidate.*" The Dylan clone released an ear shattering roar. The roar was much louder than the Daizer's screech.

"Attack!" the man yelled. The Daizer started to run at the Dylan clone.

"Go get him," I said. The Dylan clone ran at the Daizer and tackled it. The Dylan clone had the Daizer pinned a few seconds later. The Daizer struggled to break free and started biting the Dylan clone, which only angered the Dylan clone. The Dylan clone put her arm on the Daizer's neck to stop the biting, loosening her grip on one of the Daizer's arms as she did. The Daizer freed its arm and dug its claws into the Dylan clone's shoulder. The Daizer screeched at the Dylan clone, as it dug its claws deeper.

The Dylan clone pushed her arm down on the Daizer's neck, brought her head closer to the Daizer's, roared, then brought her head back up and smashed the Daizer's face in, killing it instantly. The Dylan clone removed the Daizer's claws from her shoulders, reverted, and hobbled back to me.

"Th-that's not possible," the man said, stunned, "No matter, I've killed electri and taken down their 'half-brothers' before. There's nothing you can do to surprise me, I know all your moves." The man pulled a strange device out of his pocket and pointed it at the Dylan clone.

"But before I kill you, I'm going to kill your little Daizer mimic," the man said with a twisted smile. The man shot the Dylan clone with a dark beam, but nothing happened. The man's face went from a look of victory to a look of confusion. The man shot the Dylan clone again, but still nothing happened.

"Oh, did I forget to mention the Dylan is invulnerable in her current form?" I said as I created some thunder-balls.

"She may be invulnerable, but you're not," the man said as he pointed the device at me. I threw the thunder-balls at the man, but the man activated the device as the thunder-balls were in midair. The dark beam hit me on my left shoulder and I felt an intense pain. Suddenly, I felt my strength and energy start to painfully and forcefully leave my body. *Boom.* The thunder-balls exploded around the man, breaking his device and throwing him back.

Once his device was broken, my strength and energy reentered my body. The man got up and looked at me for a second, then retreated. I turned around and continued my journey, running to make up lost time. I made it to the road just as the sun was beginning to set. After making it to the road, I took off the backpack, ate a sandwich, and fed Sparks and the Dylan clone. I examined my left shoulder while Sparks and the Dylan clone ate, and noticed that where I got shot had not healed and was bleeding just a little.

I put some snow on my left shoulder and figured it'd be fine tomorrow. I got the blanket out of the backpack and leaned up against a tree. Sparks got on my right shoulder and the Dylan clone got on my lap under the blanket. The three of us were asleep within an hour.

Chapter 9: Logan

Logan was awakened by his parents at eight to go to Church. He got dressed and at eight forty four, left to Kinship Church. Because it was the early service, Logan was with his parents in the main sanctuary with Pastor Barry White. Church ended at ten, and at ten fifteen, Logan and his parents were at their house. Logan's parents prepared the house for some family friends, while Logan prepared himself for the beast that was on its way.

Logan decided at twelve thirty one to tell his parents about the beast and his brother's plan to stop a car wreck. When Logan finished explaining everything at twelve forty, his parents thought he had lost his mind. Then, six minutes after one, there was a loud screech outside. Logan's dad went outside to investigate, and ran back inside a few seconds later. Logan got his grandmother's dog and took her outside.

"*Stronghold,*" said Logan. The dog morphed into a six foot, muscular hulk. Logan heard another screech. Logan turned and saw the beast. It was about six feet tall, was muscular, had a nightmarish face with a mouthful of fangs, and was covered in bloodstained fur. Logan remembered his brother telling him a keyword, but couldn't remember what it was.

"That thing is pretty intimidating," Logan said to himself, "Wait a second, Dylan, *Intimidate.*" Dylan unleashed a roar seven times louder than the beast's screech. The beast ran at Dylan and tackled her. The beast tried to pin Dylan, but Dylan was stronger and managed to throw the beast off of her. The beast ran at Dylan again, but this time instead tackling Dylan, the beast grabbed Dylan and threw her into one of the cars.

Dylan got up and picked up the car she was thrown into. She threw the car at the beast and ran at it. The beast caught the car, but as it raised the car to throw it back, Dylan grabbed the beast and threw it into a tree. The impact was so great that the tree snapped and fell onto the other car. The beast got up and ran towards Dylan. Dylan broke a large branch off the fallen tree, and held it like a baseball bat. The beast got close to Dylan, Dylan swung her branch, and with a bang, the beast flew away from Logan's house.

Chapter 10: Micheal

I awoke to the sound of Sparks clicking at 10:15 am. I got up and quickly ate the last sandwich. Once I was finished with the sandwich, I packed the blanket into the backpack. I put the backpack on, and switched to my electro sight. I quickly spotted the black-ts. I ran to where the black-ts were to find not one, but six wires. I took care of the black-ts, switched back to my human vision, and started cutting the wires.

"Hey, what do you think you're doing?" asked a voice from behind me. I turned around and saw Lucius, the member of Siphe. *That's not good.* I quickly shot him with a bolt of lightning and went back to cutting the wires. I was down to two wires when I felt two hands grab me from behind and pull me away.

"LET ME GO!!" I yelled.

"I might, once the car crashes," said Lucius. I quickly focused plasma into my eyes, and cut one of the wires using my laser sight. Then, before I could cut the last wire, Lucius turned me around and looked me in the eyes, as he stabbed me in the chest. He released me, and I fell to my knees, clutching the handle of the knife. *Strange, the pain I'm feeling is not a stabbing pain in my chest, but instead a pain in my bones similar to the fusion of the Orb of Conduct.*

"Oh, look at that, right on time," Lucius said. I looked behind me and saw the car approaching the wire. With my laser sight, I shot the final wire as the car made contact with it. Then, the unpredictable happened. The wire stuck to the car, causing it to act as a pendulum and rotate around the tree the wire was attached to. My heart sank as the car slid across the icy road and slammed into a tree.

Forgetting about the knife, I got up and ran towards the wrecked car. The driver's side door opened as I arrived and I saw a familiar face. It was Max, a close friend of my family. *Max? Duh, his family use to hang out with my family all the time, until about a year ago, when they started getting stalked.* I helped him, his wife Sandra, and his daughter Layla out of the car. *I might not have prevented the wreck, but at least no one died.*

"Quick, we have to get to safety," I said.

"What happened to your shoulder?" Max asked. Suddenly, a gunshot rang out from behind me and Sandra fell to the ground.

"Mom!!" Layla screamed. Another gunshot rang out and Max fell to the ground. I turned around and saw Lucius holding a gun.

"Looks like-," Lucius started, "Wait, didn't I stab you?" I looked where I had gotten stabbed and the knife was gone. There wasn't even a hole or blood, as if I had never been stabbed in the first place. I looked back up at Lucius, who had put the gun away.

"Look, seeing as how you survived the stabbing, I'll let you live as a battery if you give me the girl," Lucius said, "Deal?"

"Let me think about it," I said as I took off the backpack. I got Sparks and the Dylan clone out of my coat and took it off. Once the coat was off, I charged the electro armor.

"I'm going to take that as a 'no'," Lucius said as he pointed at my left shoulder with a device similar to the one that shot me yesterday. However, instead of a dark beam coming from it, a dark light radiated from its end. All of a sudden, my strength and energy began to painfully and forcefully leave my body. I fell to my knees and Lucius deactivated the device. I managed to look up at Lucius and saw him staring back at me with a villainous smile. *Déjà vu.*

"You half-brothers are so predictable," Lucius said as he pulled out an odd gun-looking thing and pointed it at Layla, "It's unnatural how much you are willing to lay down your lives for others. Sadly for you, your life will be laid down in vain." A small dart shot out from the gun-looking thing and hit Layla in the neck. Layla collapsed a few seconds later and Lucius reactivated the device.

Pain surged through my body as my strength and energy was siphoned. *The mimic crystal might help, but it's in the backpack. How am I supposed to get to it?* Then, snow hit Lucius in the back of the head. He looked behind him and nearly jumped out of his skin. Standing behind him was the Dylan clone in her powerful form.

"In-*Intimidate*," I said weakly. The Dylan clone unleashed a roar much louder than yesterday's. The roar interfered with the device and caused it to shut down. While Lucius tried to get the device back on, I gathered the last of my strength and crawled to the backpack. Once at the backpack, I searched and found the mimic crystal. As soon as my skin made contact with the mimic crystal, my strength and energy returned. Though my strength and energy had returned, I felt sore and stiff. I stumbled as I got up, and looked at Lucius.

"You still think you can win?" Lucius asked as he pointed the device at me. The dark light radiated from the device again, but this time, instead of feeling strength and energy leave my body, I felt the mimic crystal heat up. Suddenly, the device started to spark and glow yellow. The mimic crystal cracked like thunder, and the device exploded, throwing Lucius back a few feet. Lucius quickly got up and ran at me.

Lucius tackled me, which caused me to drop the mimic crystal. Once he had me pinned, he pulled out an odd-looking Taser. He jabbed the Taser into my side and activated it. Within seconds, I felt like I had just had the breath knocked out of me. I gasped for air, but to no avail. Everything began to fade. Then, the Dylan clone roared and ran towards Lucius and me. The Dylan clone pulled Lucius off of me and threw him behind her.

"I'll keep the girl safe," said a female voice, "So leave and go to safety." The Dylan clone lifted me up and threw me in the direction of my house. I switched to my electrical form while in midair and turned around to see the Dylan clone in her invulnerable form guarding Layla. The Dylan clone barked at Sparks, and Sparks switched to his electrical form. Sparks flew to me and I reluctantly flew back to my house.

When I arrived at the house, I made a not-so graceful landing. Once I got up, I noticed both cars were totaled, and Plasmic and Keveal were talking with my family. I switched back into my normal form, changed the electro armor back to its normal variant, and approached them.

"Are you okay?" asked Plasmic.

"Yeah, I'm okay," I said, then fainted.

Sneak Peak of The Soldier Lost

Sunday, February 15, 2009.

When the girl awoke, she was in a square concrete room. There was a single light bulb hanging from the ceiling, barely illuminating the room. To her left was a single pillow next to an old, torn blanket. To her right, a toilet and a sink. *Oh no*, the girl thought, *they've caught me*. She started to cry, when she felt something nudge her side. She looked down and saw an orange Boston terrier. Suddenly, the door opened and a woman, who had white hair yet looked younger than thirty, came in.

"I've waited a long time for this," said the woman as she approached the girl. The woman pulled out a strange metallic rod and jabbed it into the girl's shoulder. The woman pushed a button on the rod and the rod cut into the girls shoulder. The woman then pulled the rod away and touched the cut. Then, the girl began to feel weaker and weaker. She was starting to lose consciousness when the woman pulled her hand away. The girl was unconscious by the time the woman left the room.

Message from the Author

Howdy, happy reader!!! Voltage here. I've been writing stories since I was in the fifth grade, and have since dreamed of being an author. So far, it would seem that I'm closer to achieving that dream, and so I want to encourage you to follow your dream. No matter what life throws at you, don't give up on it. Just look at me, I've got ADHD and Asperger's, and I wrote a book! What's stopping you? Your dream only becomes impossible if you lose faith in it. Work for it, your dream won't accomplish itself. You can't do nothing at a job and get paid, you have to put effort into it. Don't go for something super easy, dream big.

Thanks, and remember, Keep Calm and Dream On!!!

Made in the USA
Columbia, SC
12 June 2022